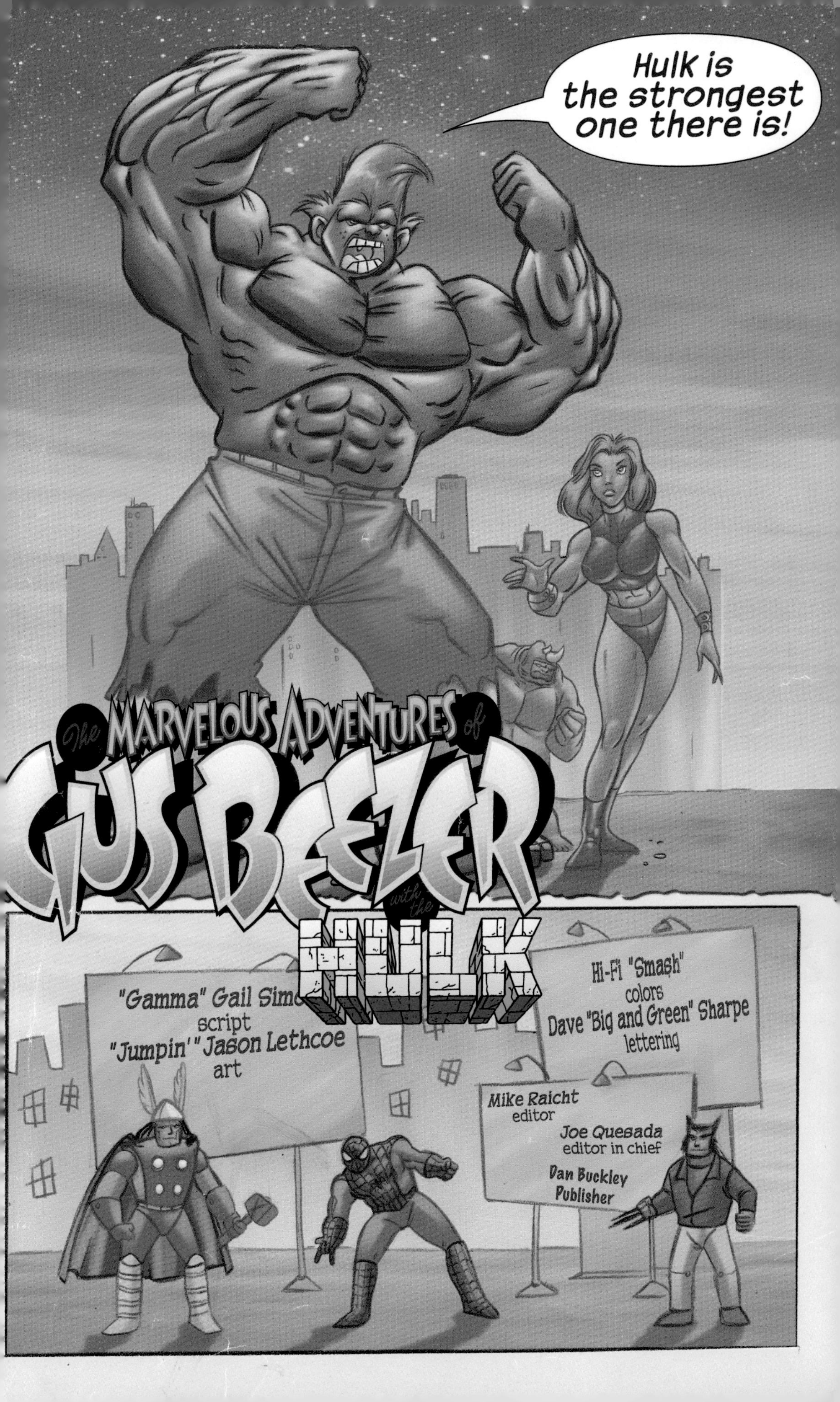

Hulk is the strongest one there is!
The MARVELOUS ADVENTURES of
GUS BEEZER
with the
HULK
"Gamma" Gail Sim
script
"Jumpin'" Jason Lethcoe
art
Hi-Fi "Smash"
colors
Dave "Big and Green" Sharpe
lettering
Mike Raicht
editor
Joe Quesada
editor in chief
Dan Buckley
Publisher

VISIT US AT
www.abdopub.com

Spotlight, a division of ABDO Publishing Company Inc., is the school and library distributor of the Marvel Entertainment books.

Library bound edition © 2006

Library of Congress Cataloging-in-Publication Data

Gus Beezer With the Hulk

ISBN 1-59961-049-3   (Reinforced Library Bound Edition)

All Spotlight books are reinforced library binding and manufactured in the United States of America

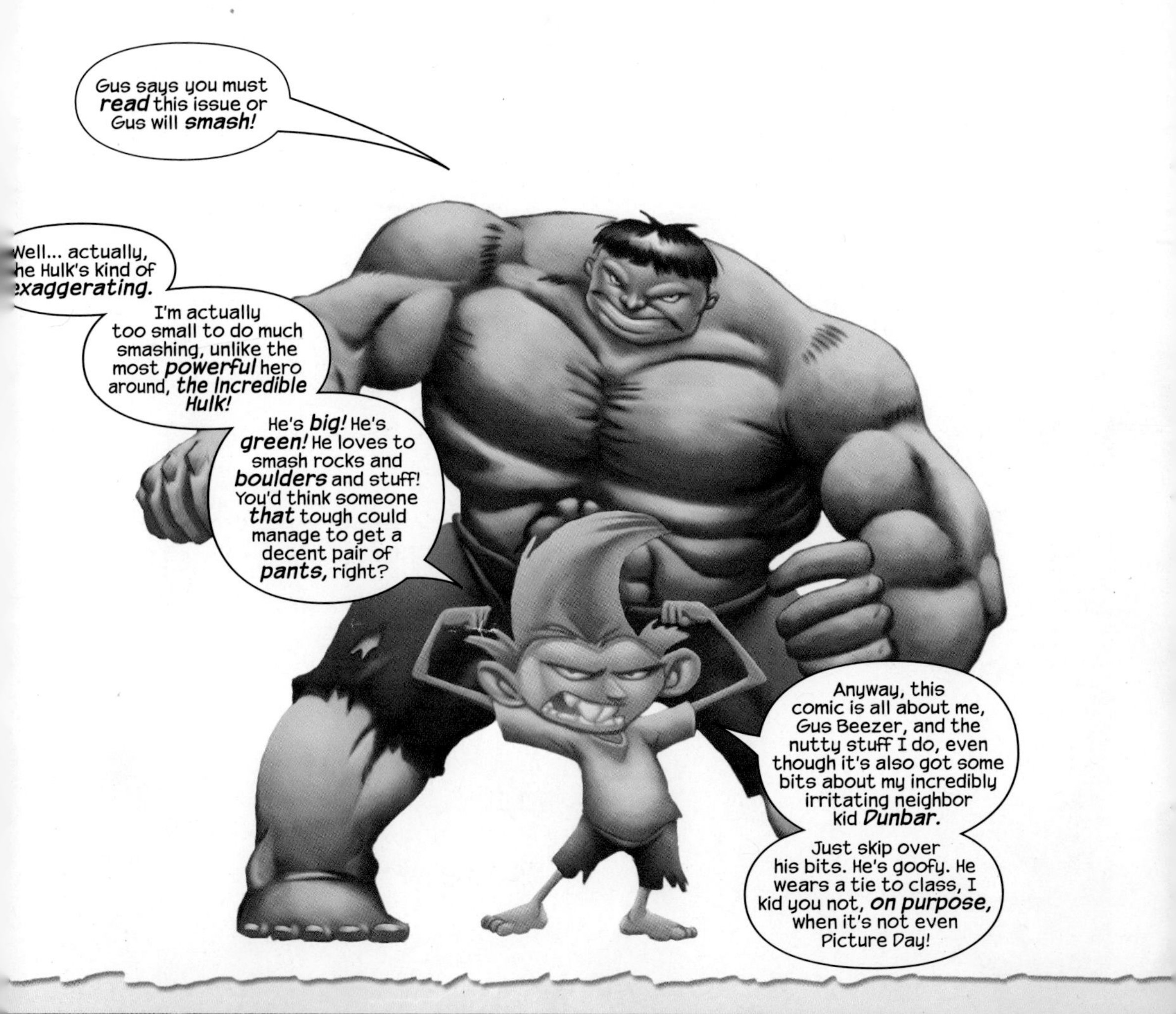
Gus says you must read this issue or Gus will smash!
Well... actually, he Hulk's kind of xaggerating.
I'm actually too small to do much smashing, unlike the most powerful hero around, the Incredible Hulk!
He's big! He's green! He loves to smash rocks and boulders and stuff! You'd think someone that tough could manage to get a decent pair of pants, right?
Anyway, this comic is all about me, Gus Beezer, and the nutty stuff I do, even though it's also got some bits about my incredibly irritating neighbor kid Dunbar.
Just skip over his bits. He's goofy. He wears a tie to class, I kid you not, on purpose, when it's not even Picture Day!

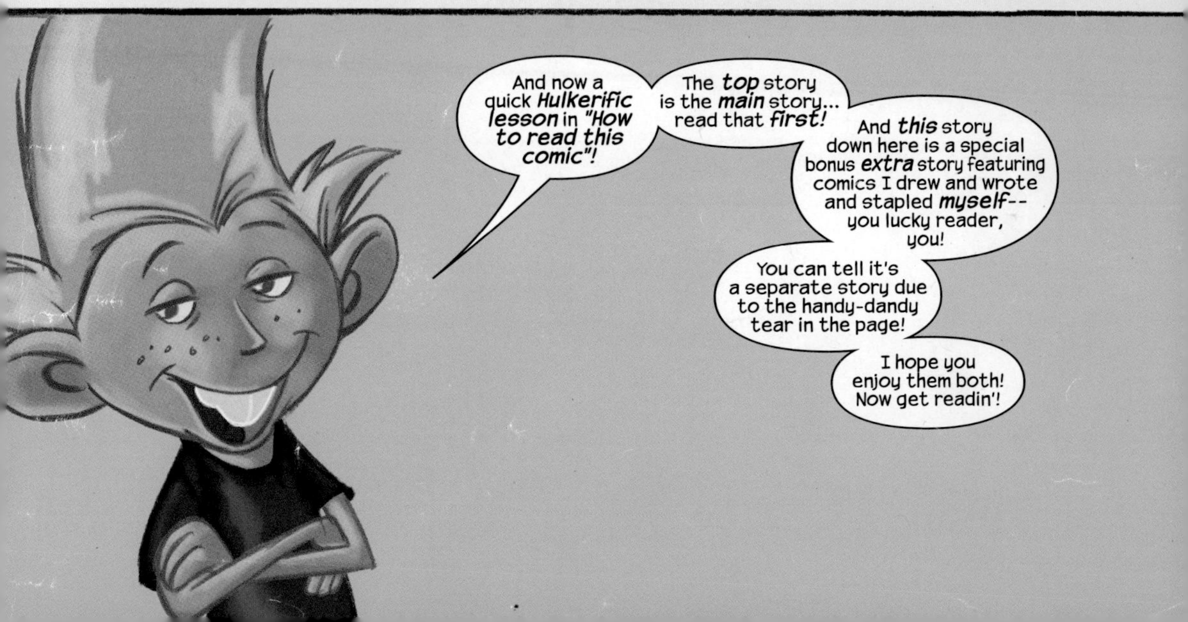
And now a quick Hulkerific lesson in "How to read this comic"!
The top story is the main story... read that first!
And this story down here is a special bonus extra story featuring comics I drew and wrote and stapled myself-- you lucky reader, you!
You can tell it's a separate story due to the handy-dandy tear in the page!
I hope you enjoy them both! Now get readin'!

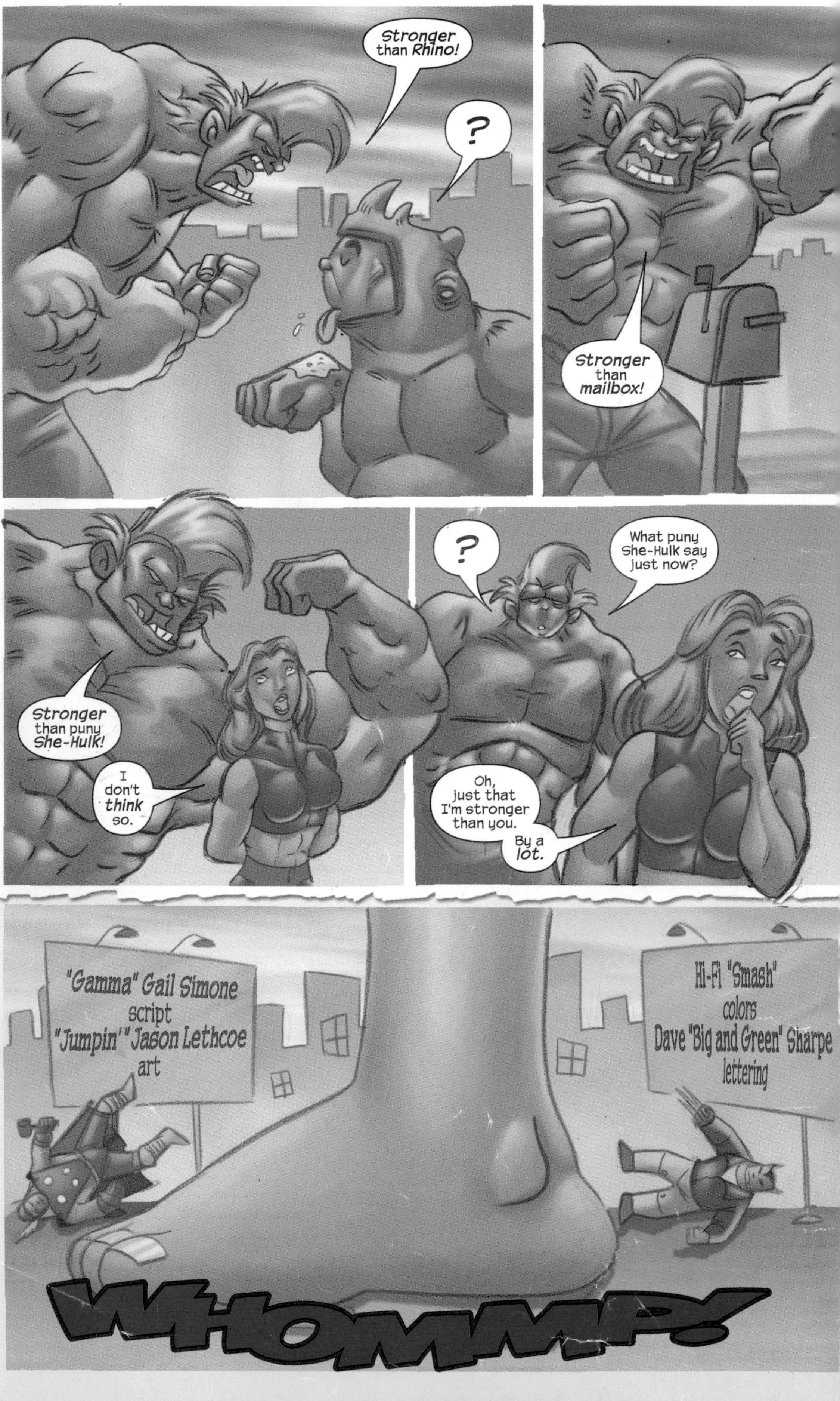
Stronger than Rhino!
?
Stronger than mailbox!
Stronger than puny She-Hulk!
I don't think so.
?
What puny She-Hulk say just now?
Oh, just that I'm stronger than you.
By a lot.
"Gamma" Gail Simone script "Jumpin'" Jason Lethcoe art
Hi-Fi "Smash" colors Dave "Big and Green" Sharpe lettering
WHOMMP!

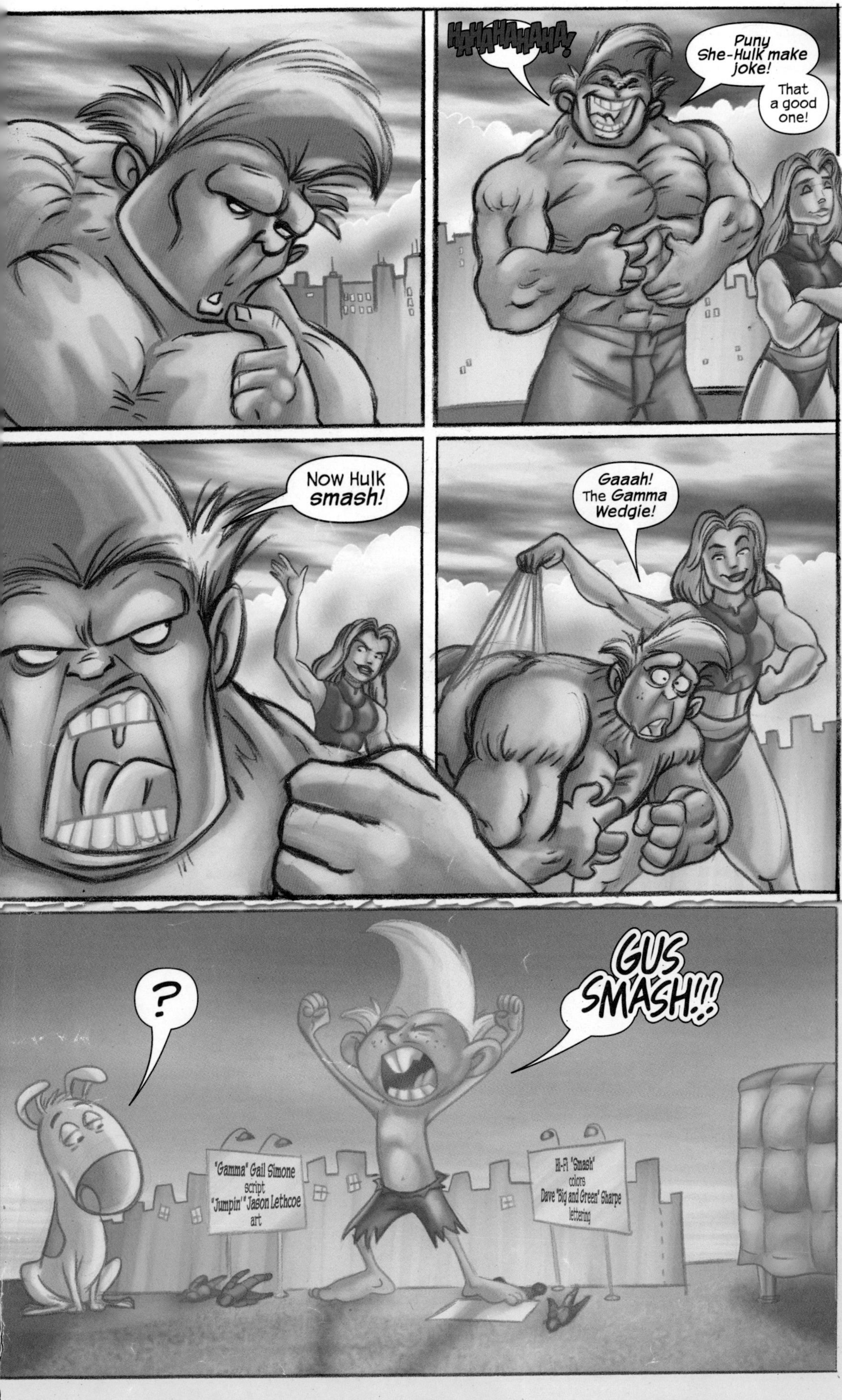
HAHAHAHAHAHA!
Puny She-Hulk make joke!
That a good one!
Now Hulk smash!
Gaaah! The Gamma Wedgie!
?
GUS SMASH!!!
"Gamma" Gail Simone script "Jumpin'" Jason Lethcoe art
Hi-Fi "Smash" colors Dave "Big and Green" Sharpe lettering

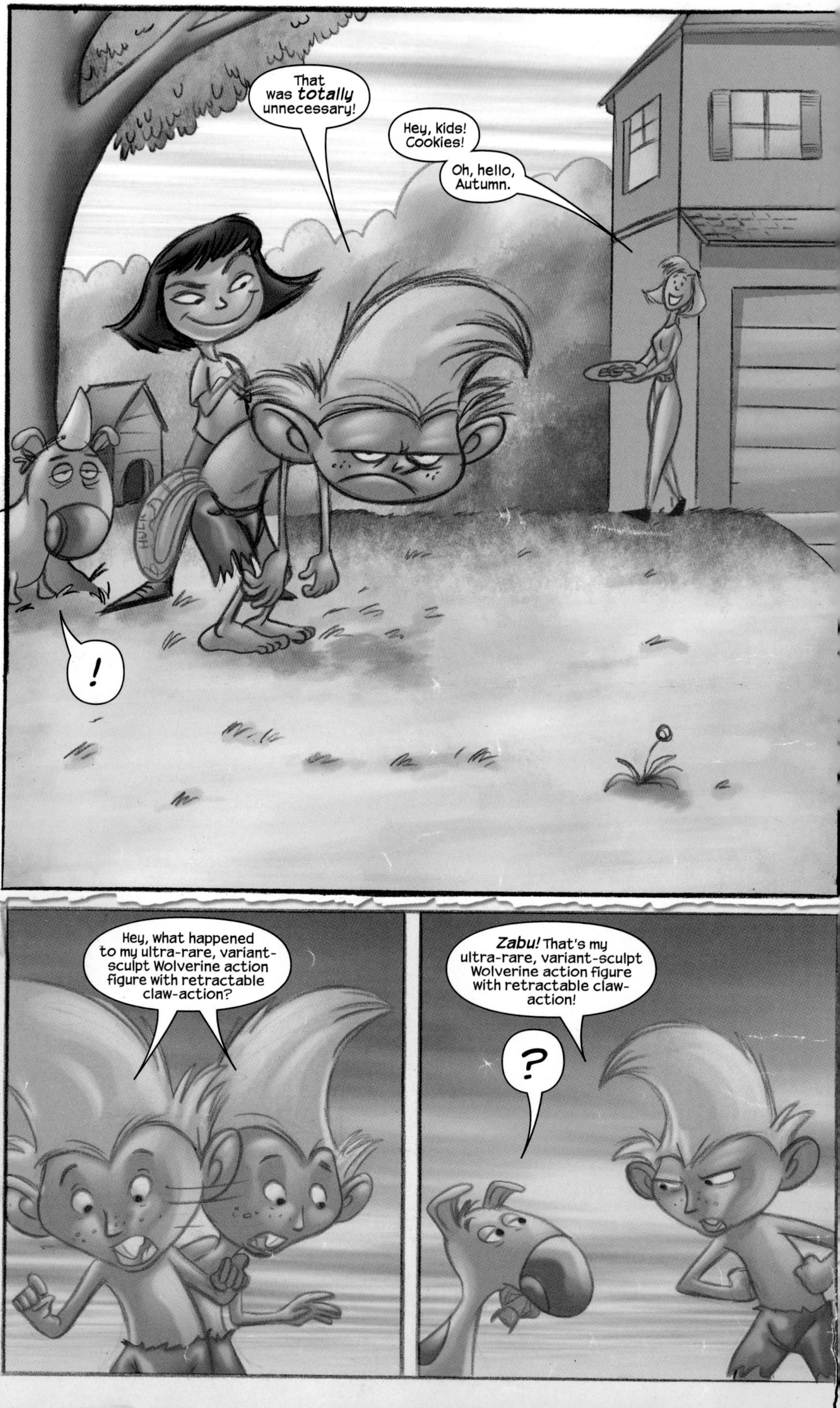
That was *totally* unnecessary!
Hey, kids! Cookies!
Oh, hello, Autumn.
HULK
!
Hey, what happened to my ultra-rare, variant-sculpt Wolverine action figure with retractable claw-action?
Zabu! That's my ultra-rare, variant-sculpt Wolverine action figure with retractable claw-action!
?

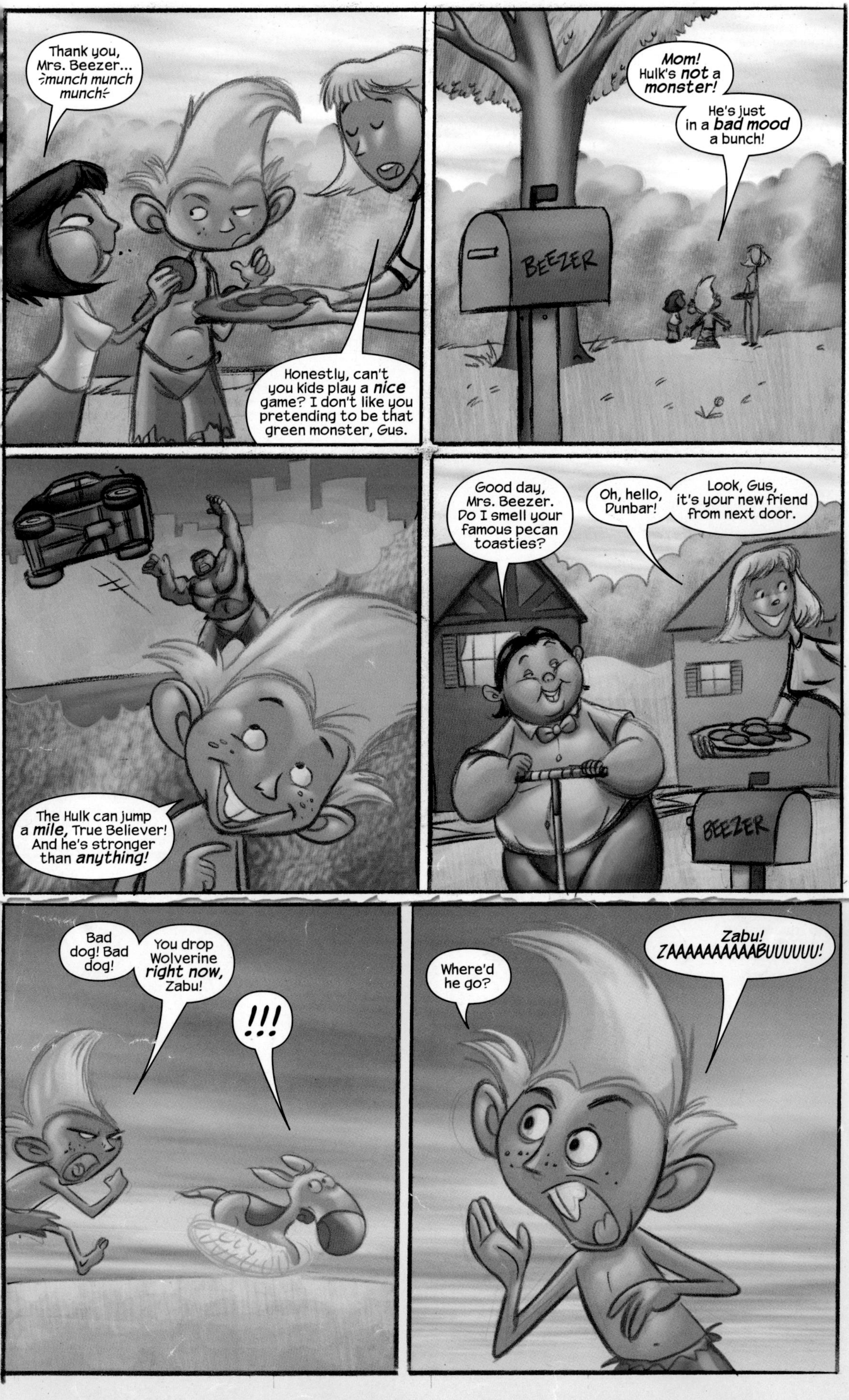
Thank you, Mrs. Beezer... ⩦munch munch munch⩦
Honestly, can't you kids play a *nice* game? I don't like you pretending to be that green monster, Gus.
Mom! Hulk's *not* a *monster!*
He's just in a *bad mood* a bunch!
BEEZER
The Hulk can jump a *mile,* True Believer! And he's stronger than *anything!*
Good day, Mrs. Beezer. Do I smell your famous pecan toasties?
Oh, hello, Dunbar!
Look, Gus, it's your new friend from next door.
BEEZER
Bad dog! Bad dog!
You drop Wolverine *right now,* Zabu!
!!!
Where'd he go?
Zabu! ZAAAAAAAAAABUUUUUU!

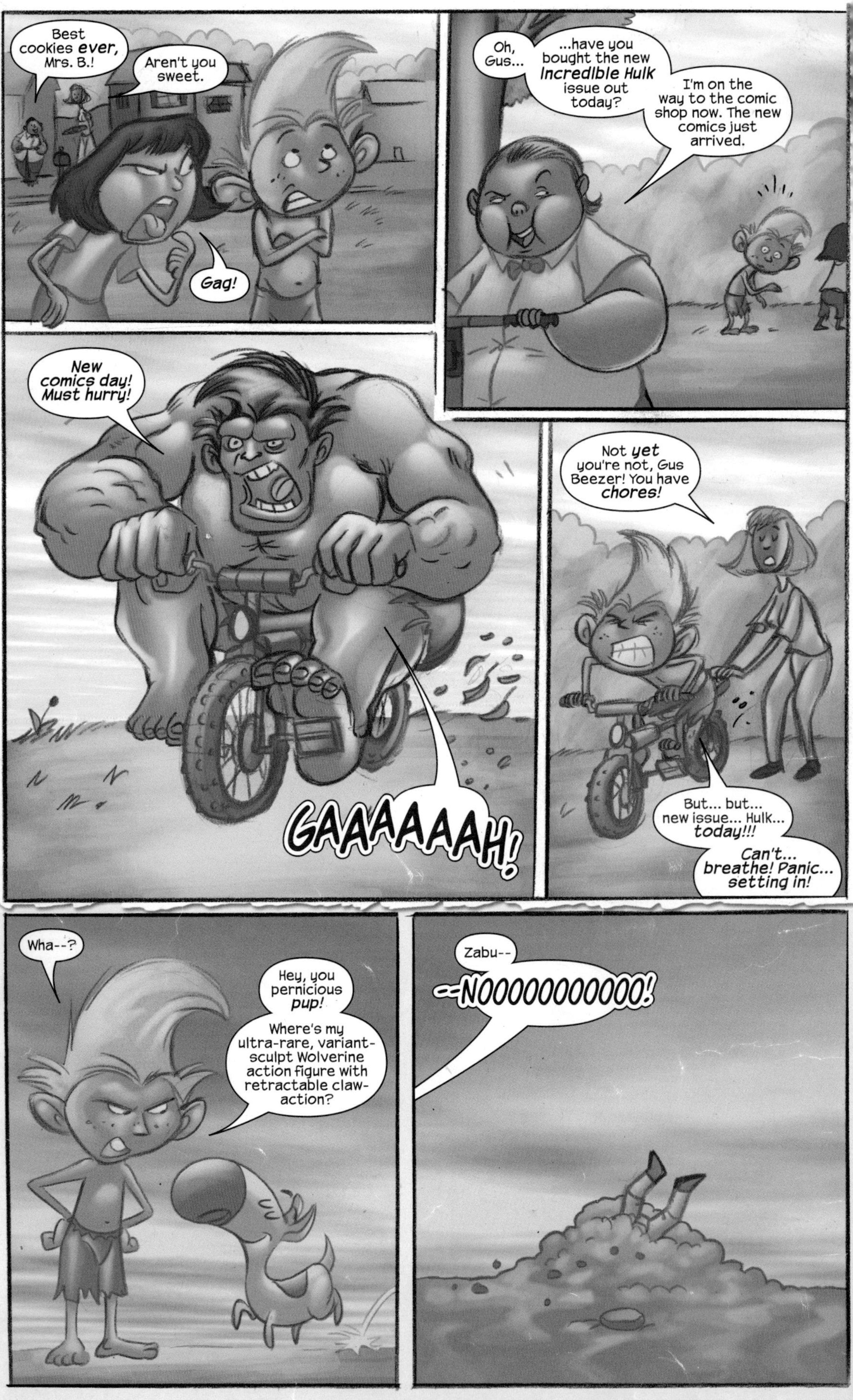
Best cookies ever, Mrs. B.!
Aren't you sweet.
Gag!
Oh, Gus...
...have you bought the new Incredible Hulk issue out today?
I'm on the way to the comic shop now. The new comics just arrived.
New comics day! Must hurry!
GAAAAAAH!
Not yet you're not, Gus Beezer! You have chores!
But... but... new issue... Hulk... today!!!
Can't... breathe! Panic... setting in!
Wha--?
Hey, you pernicious pup!
Where's my ultra-rare, variant-sculpt Wolverine action figure with retractable claw-action?
Zabu--
--NOOOOOOOOOOO!

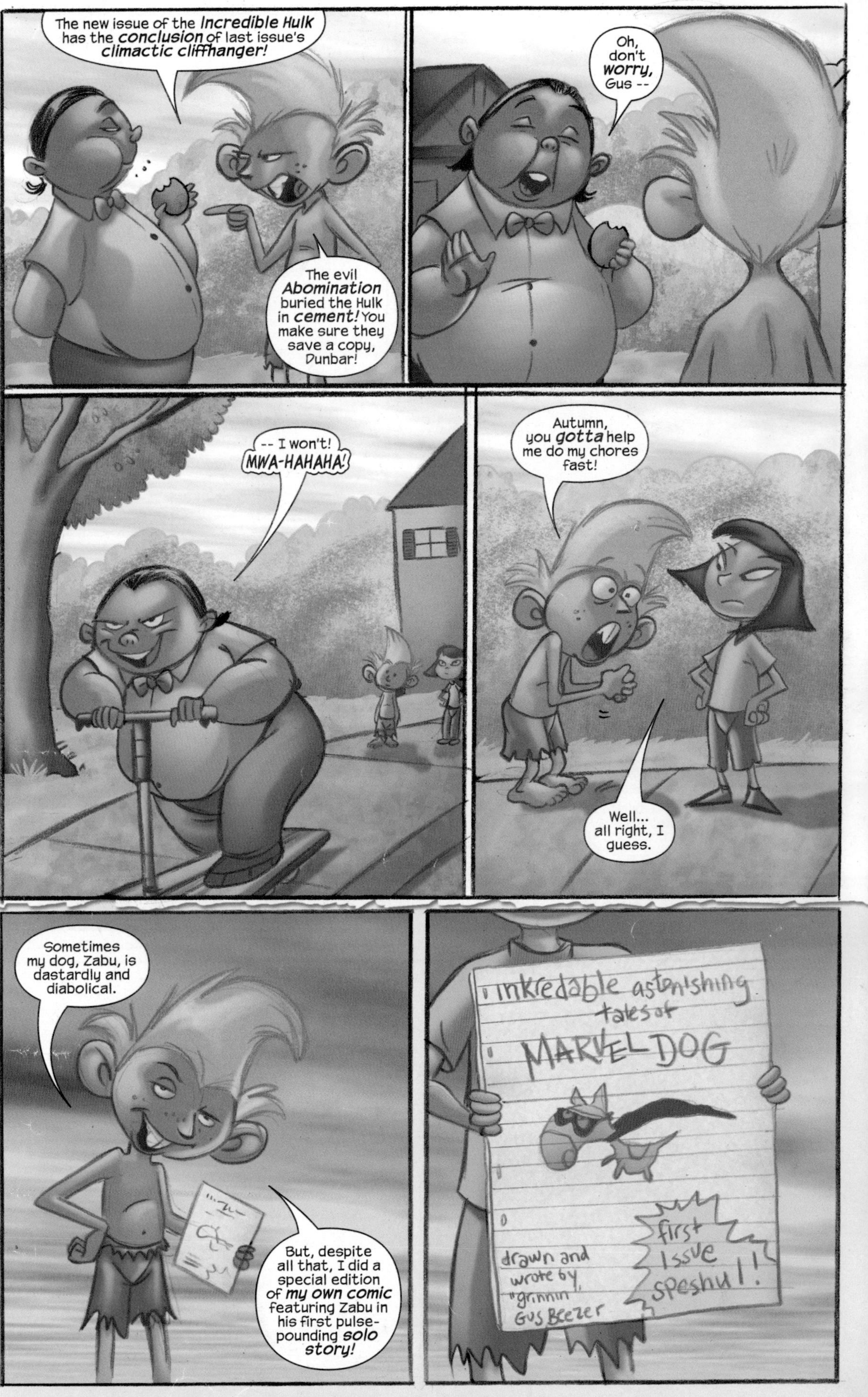

The new issue of the Incredible Hulk has the conclusion of last issue's climactic cliffhanger!
The evil Abomination buried the Hulk in cement! You make sure they save a copy, Dunbar!
Oh, don't worry, Gus --
-- I won't! MWA-HAHAHA!
Autumn, you gotta help me do my chores fast!
Well... all right, I guess.
Sometimes my dog, Zabu, is dastardly and diabolical.
But, despite all that, I did a special edition of my own comic featuring Zabu in his first pulse-pounding solo story!
inkredable astonishing tales of
MARVEL DOG
drawn and wrote by "grinnin Gus Beezer
first issue speshul!

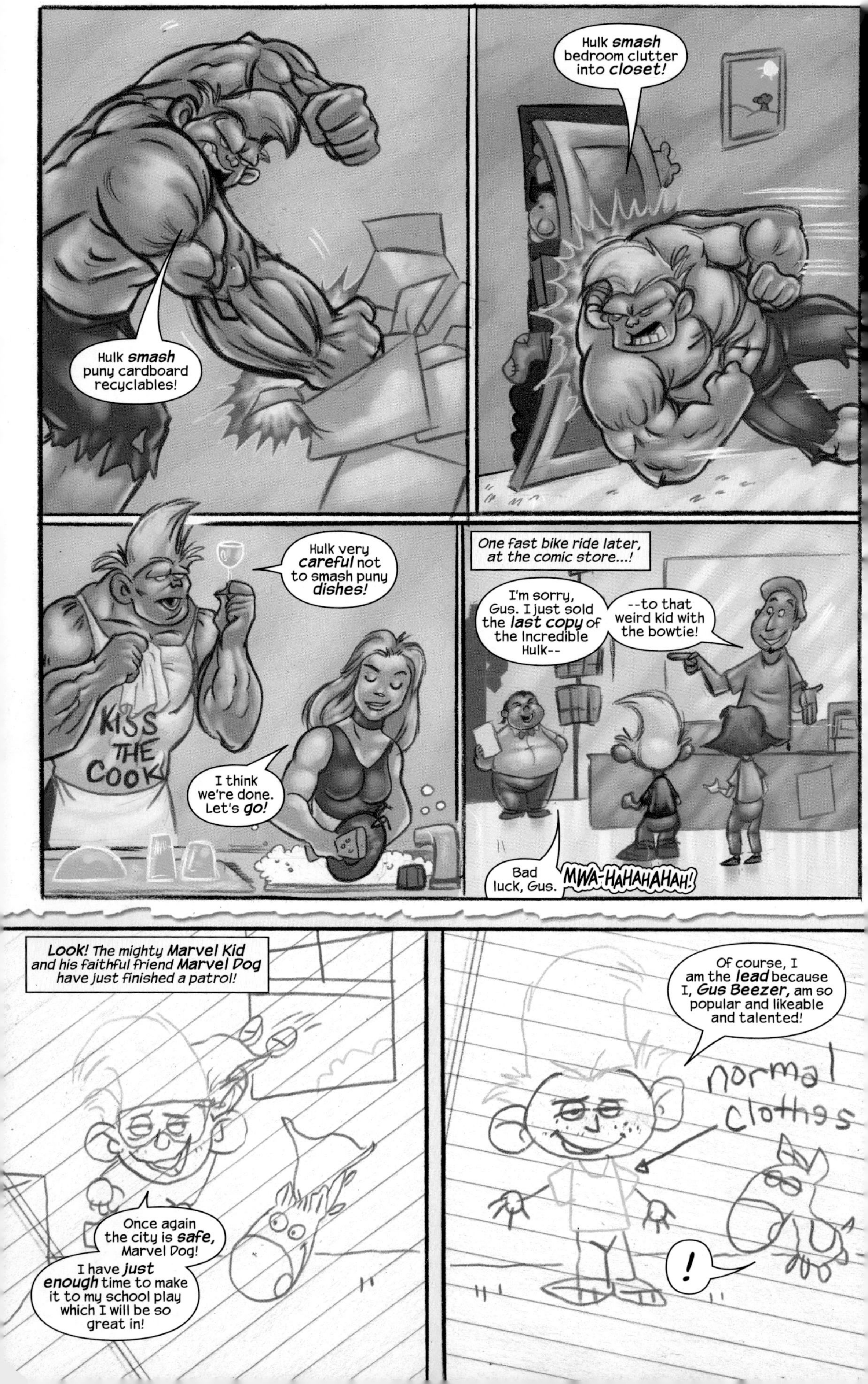
Hulk smash puny cardboard recyclables!
Hulk smash bedroom clutter into closet!
Hulk very careful not to smash puny dishes!
I think we're done. Let's go!
One fast bike ride later, at the comic store...!
I'm sorry, Gus. I just sold the last copy of the Incredible Hulk--
--to that weird kid with the bowtie!
Bad luck, Gus.
MWA-HAHAHAHAH!
Look! The mighty Marvel Kid and his faithful friend Marvel Dog have just finished a patrol!
Once again the city is safe, Marvel Dog!
I have just enough time to make it to my school play which I will be so great in!
Of course, I am the lead because I, Gus Beezer, am so popular and likeable and talented!
normal clothes
!

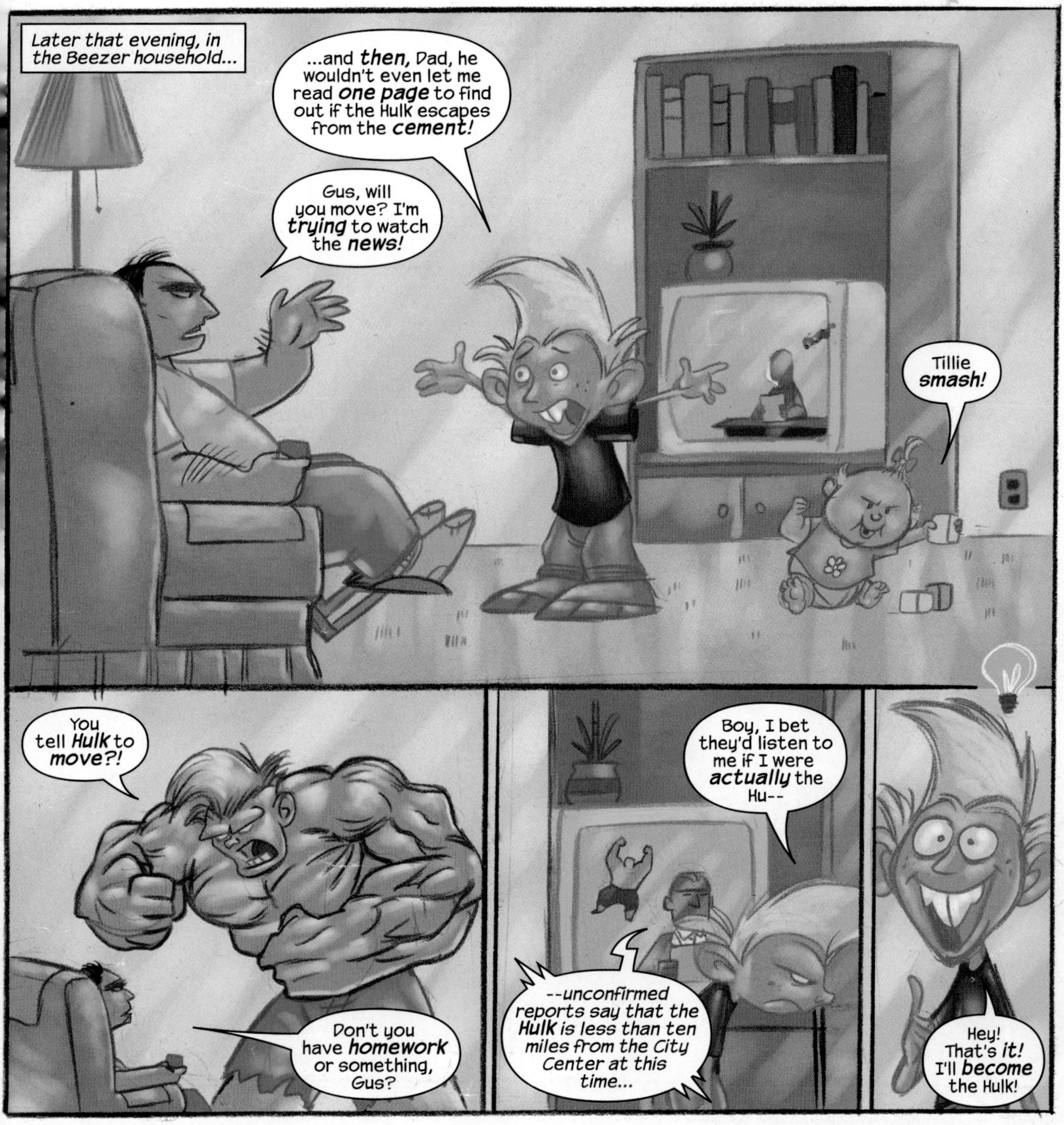
Later that evening, in the Beezer household...
...and then, Dad, he wouldn't even let me read one page to find out if the Hulk escapes from the cement!
Gus, will you move? I'm trying to watch the news!
Tillie smash!
You tell Hulk to move?!
Don't you have homework or something, Gus?
Boy, I bet they'd listen to me if I were actually the Hu--
--unconfirmed reports say that the Hulk is less than ten miles from the City Center at this time...
Hey! That's it! I'll become the Hulk!

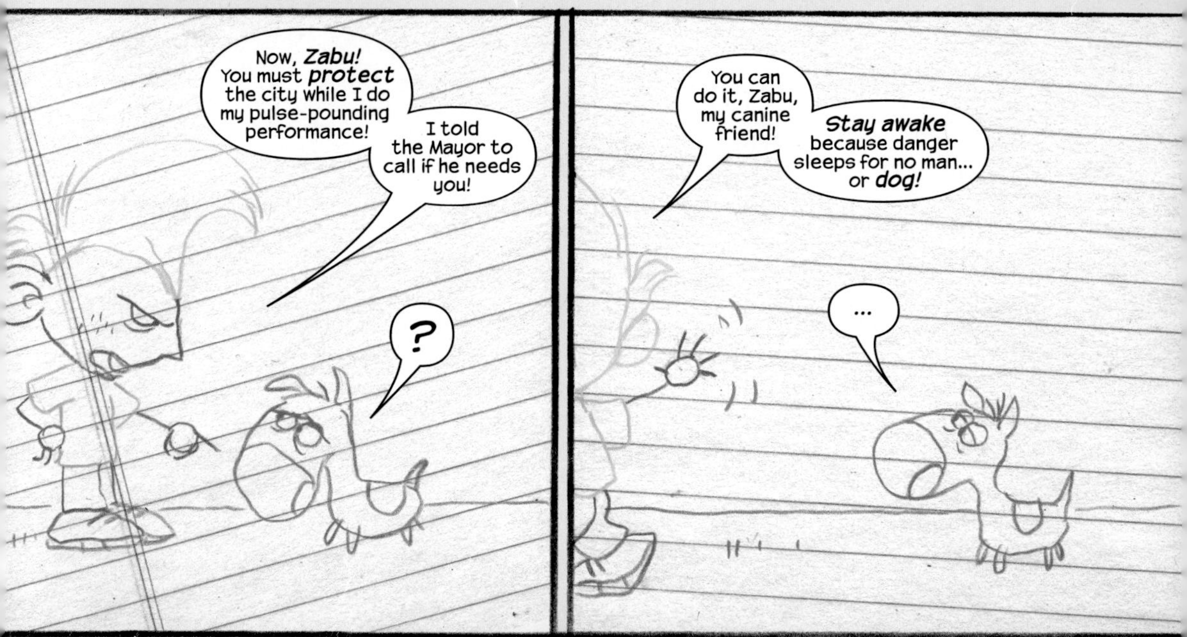
Now, Zabu! You must protect the city while I do my pulse-pounding performance!
I told the Mayor to call if he needs you!
?
You can do it, Zabu, my canine friend!
Stay awake because danger sleeps for no man... or dog!
...

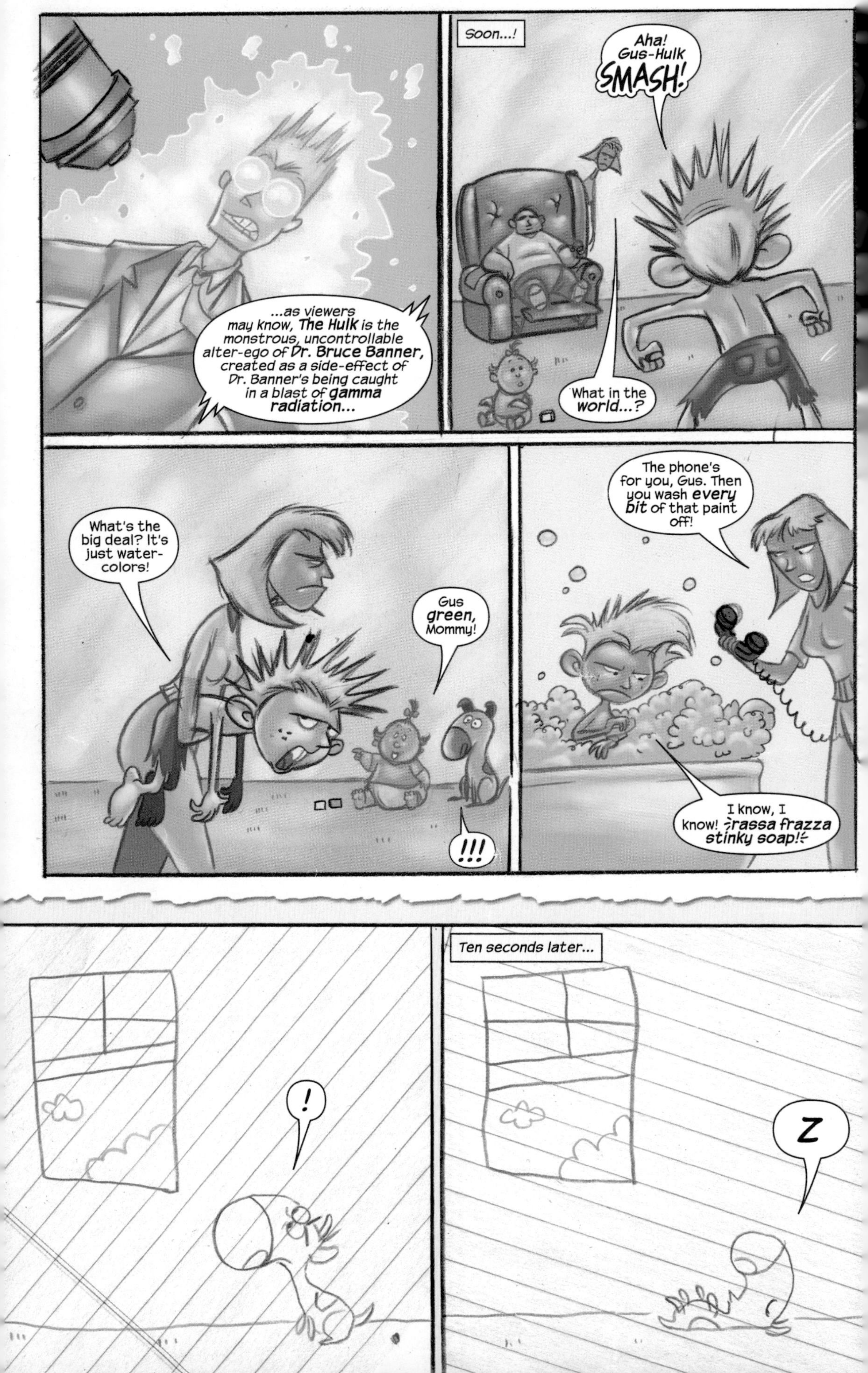
...as viewers may know, The Hulk is the monstrous, uncontrollable alter-ego of Dr. Bruce Banner, created as a side-effect of Dr. Banner's being caught in a blast of gamma radiation...
Soon...!
Aha! Gus-Hulk SMASH!
What in the world...?
What's the big deal? It's just water-colors!
Gus green, Mommy!
!!!
The phone's for you, Gus. Then you wash every bit of that paint off!
I know, I know! rassa frazza stinky soap!
!
Ten seconds later...
Z

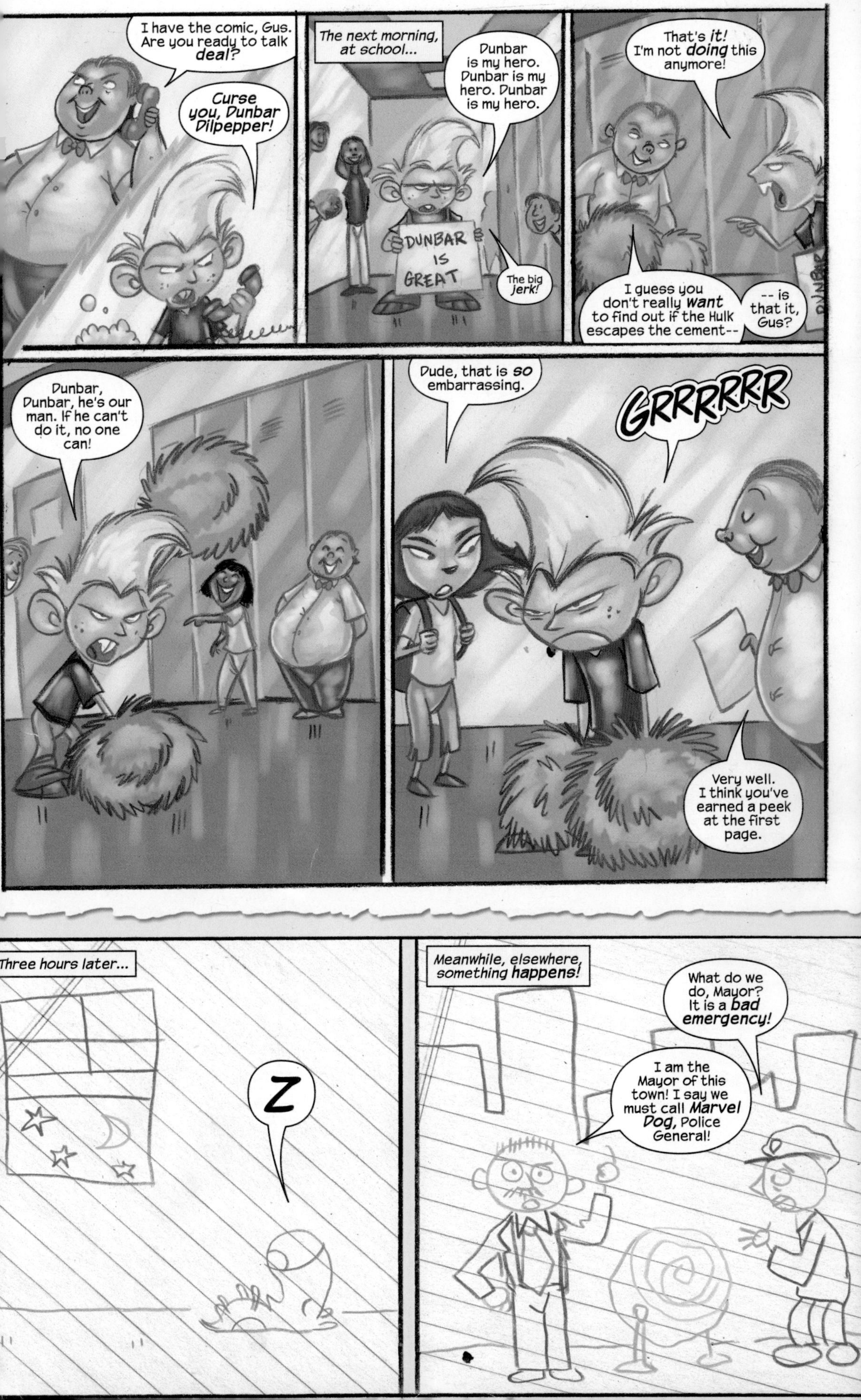
I have the comic, Gus. Are you ready to talk deal?
Curse you, Dunbar Dilpepper!
The next morning, at school...
Dunbar is my hero. Dunbar is my hero. Dunbar is my hero.
DUNBAR IS GREAT
The big jerk!
That's it! I'm not doing this anymore!
I guess you don't really want to find out if the Hulk escapes the cement--
-- is that it, Gus?
Dunbar, Dunbar, he's our man. If he can't do it, no one can!
Dude, that is so embarrassing.
GRRRRRR
Very well. I think you've earned a peek at the first page.
Three hours later...
Z
Meanwhile, elsewhere, something happens!
What do we do, Mayor? It is a bad emergency!
I am the Mayor of this town! I say we must call Marvel Dog, Police General!

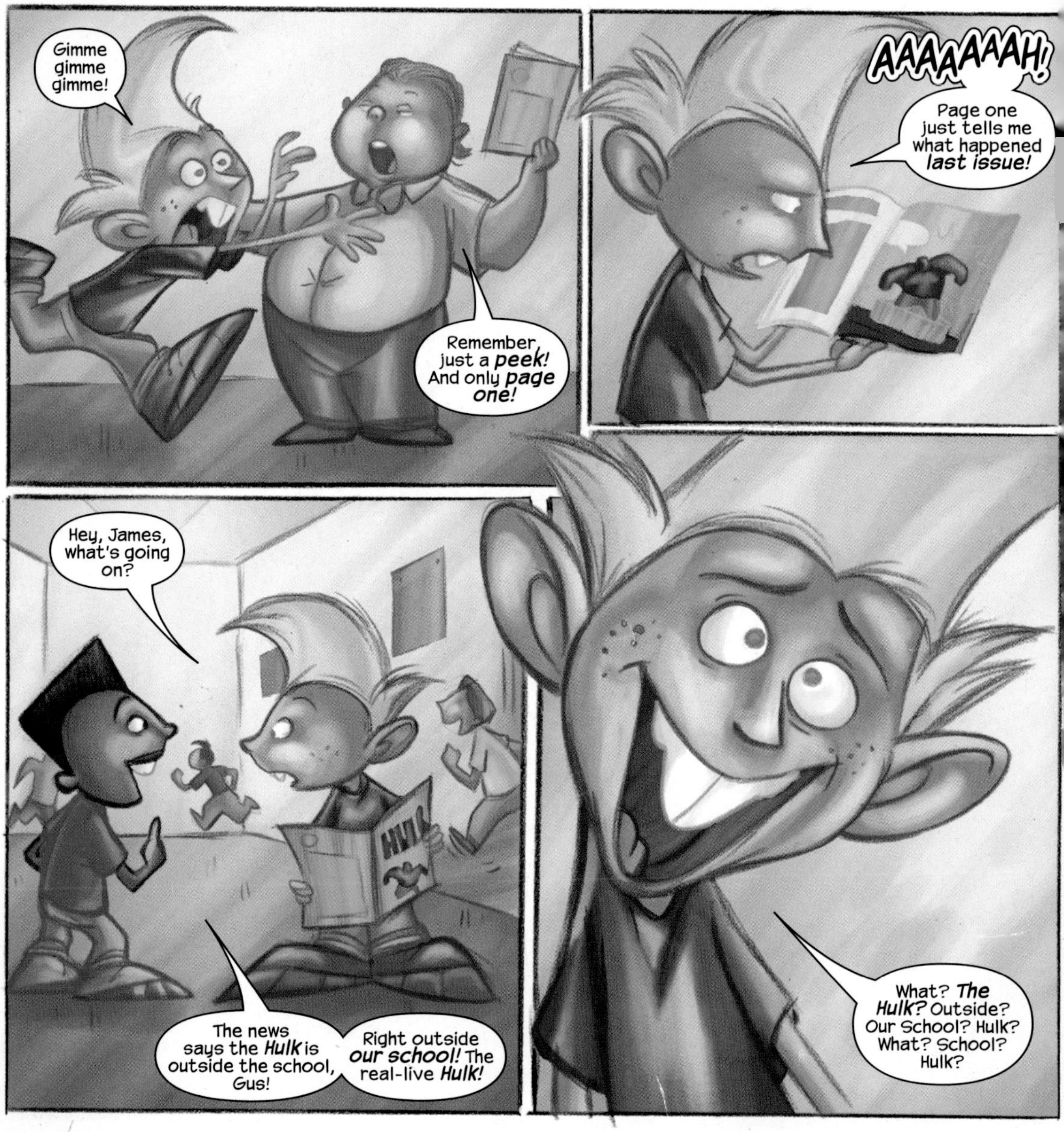
Gimme gimme gimme!
Remember, just a peek! And only page one!
AAAAAAAH!
Page one just tells me what happened last issue!
Hey, James, what's going on?
The news says the Hulk is outside the school, Gus!
Right outside our school! The real-live Hulk!
What? The Hulk? Outside? Our School? Hulk? What? School? Hulk?

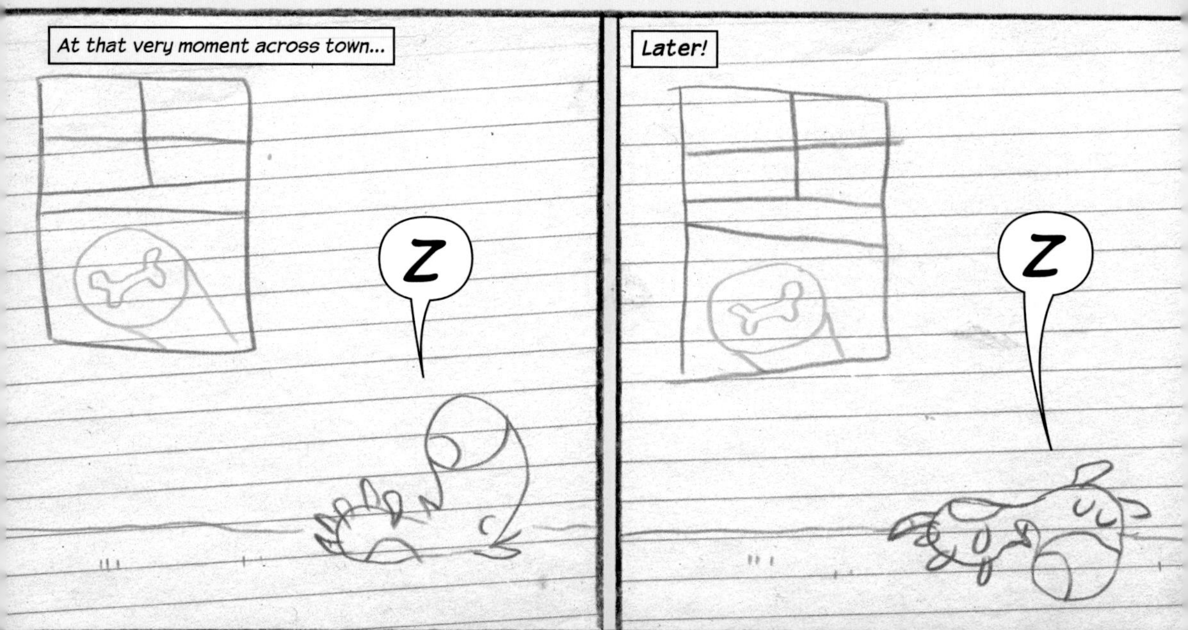
At that very moment across town...
Z
Later!
Z

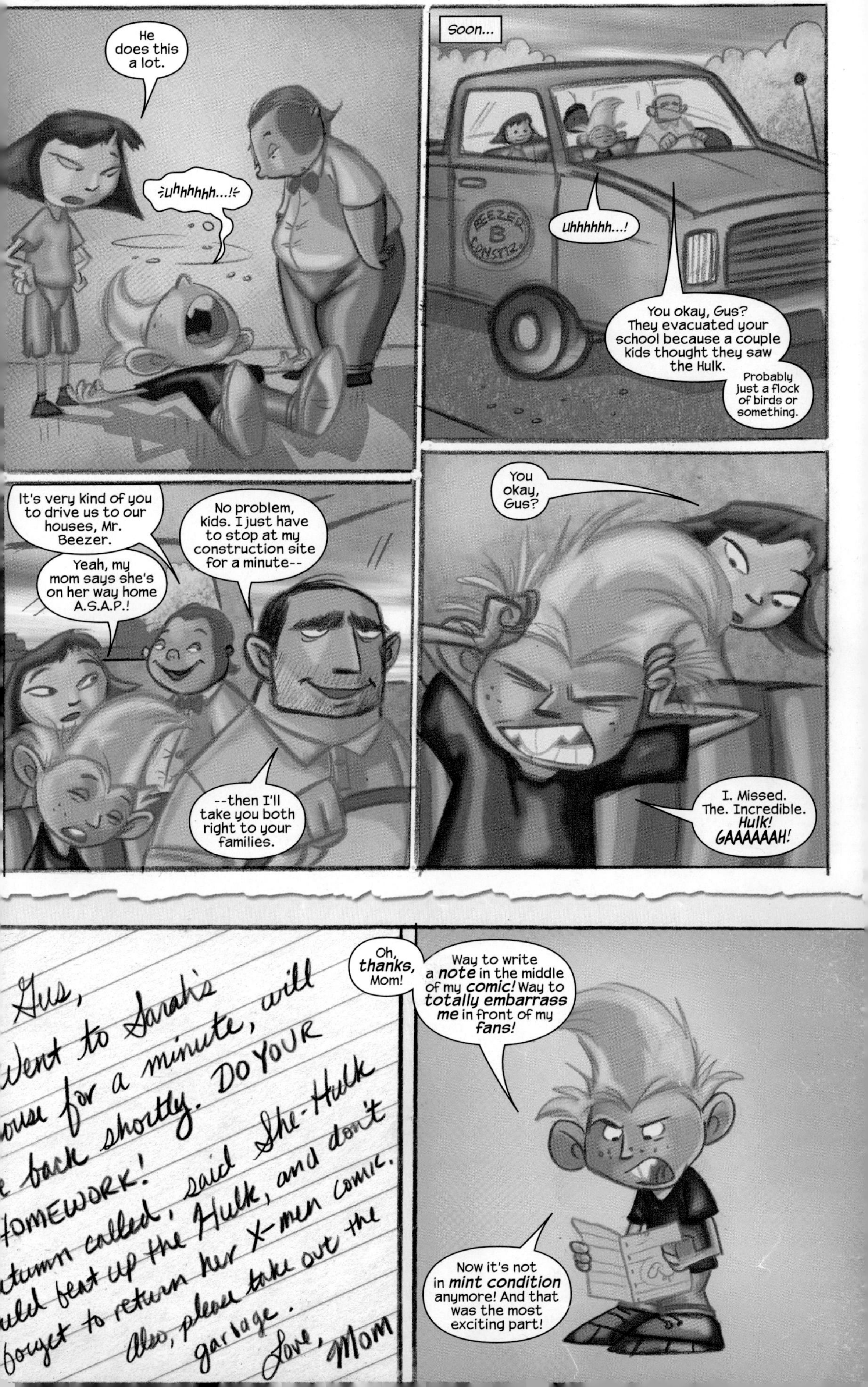
He does this a lot.
Uhhhhhh...!
Soon...
Uhhhhhh...!
You okay, Gus? They evacuated your school because a couple kids thought they saw the Hulk.
Probably just a flock of birds or something.
It's very kind of you to drive us to our houses, Mr. Beezer.
Yeah, my mom says she's on her way home A.S.A.P.!
No problem, kids. I just have to stop at my construction site for a minute--
--then I'll take you both right to your families.
You okay, Gus?
I. Missed. The. Incredible. Hulk! GAAAAAAH!
Gus,
Went to Sarah's
ouse for a minute, will
back shortly. DO YOUR
OMEWORK!
utumn called, said She-Hulk
uld beat up the Hulk, and don't
forget to return her X-men comic.
Also, please take out the
garage.
Love,
Mom
Oh, thanks, Mom!
Way to write a note in the middle of my comic! Way to totally embarrass me in front of my fans!
Now it's not in mint condition anymore! And that was the most exciting part!

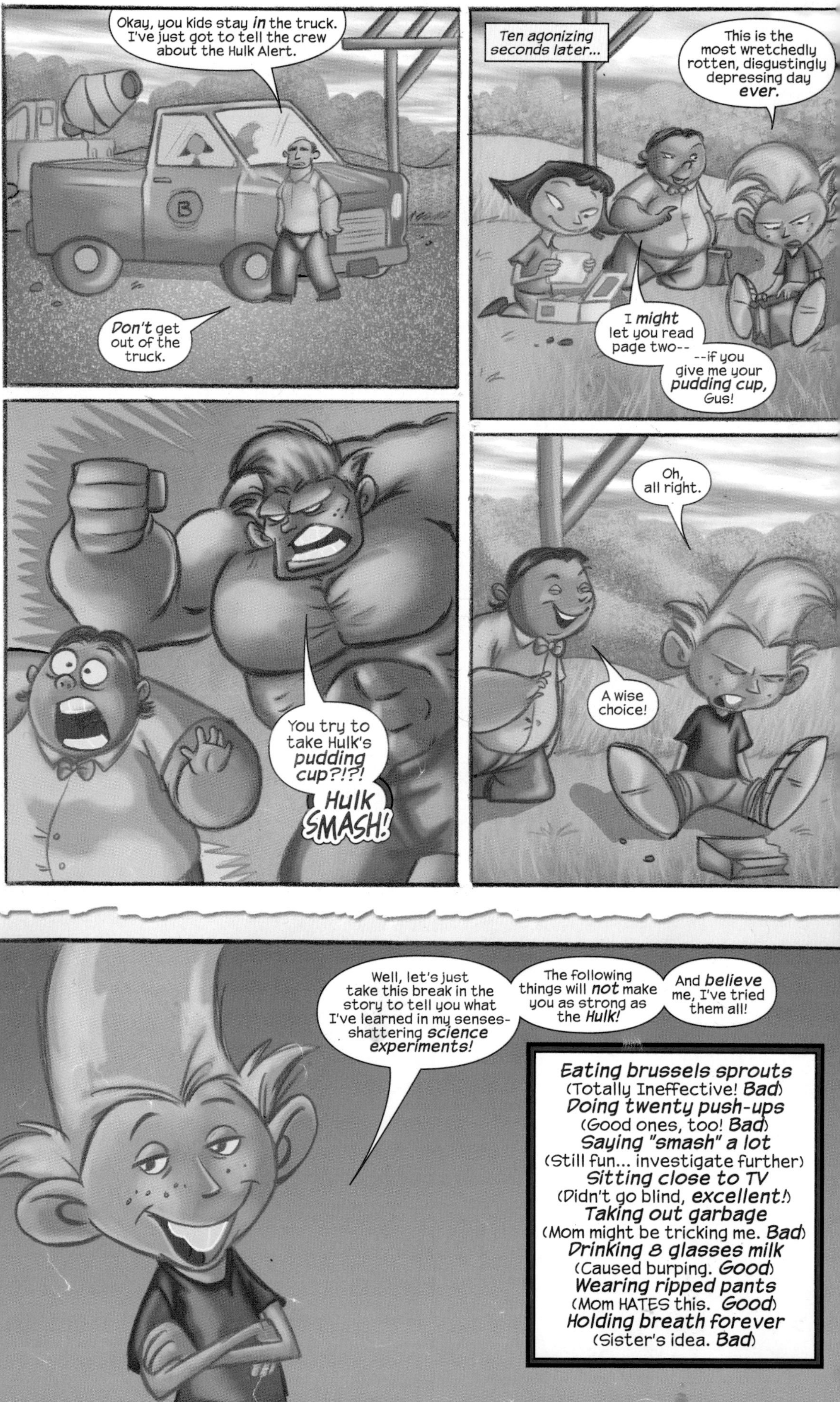
Okay, you kids stay in the truck. I've just got to tell the crew about the Hulk Alert.
Don't get out of the truck.
Ten agonizing seconds later...
This is the most wretchedly rotten, disgustingly depressing day ever.
I might let you read page two--
--if you give me your pudding cup, Gus!
You try to take Hulk's pudding cup?!?!
Hulk SMASH!
Oh, all right.
A wise choice!
Well, let's just take this break in the story to tell you what I've learned in my senses-shattering science experiments!
The following things will not make you as strong as the Hulk!
And believe me, I've tried them all!
Eating brussels sprouts
(Totally Ineffective! Bad)
Doing twenty push-ups
(Good ones, too! Bad)
Saying "smash" a lot
(Still fun... investigate further)
Sitting close to TV
(Didn't go blind, excellent!)
Taking out garbage
(Mom might be tricking me. Bad)
Drinking 8 glasses milk
(Caused burping. Good)
Wearing ripped pants
(Mom HATES this. Good)
Holding breath forever
(Sister's idea. Bad)

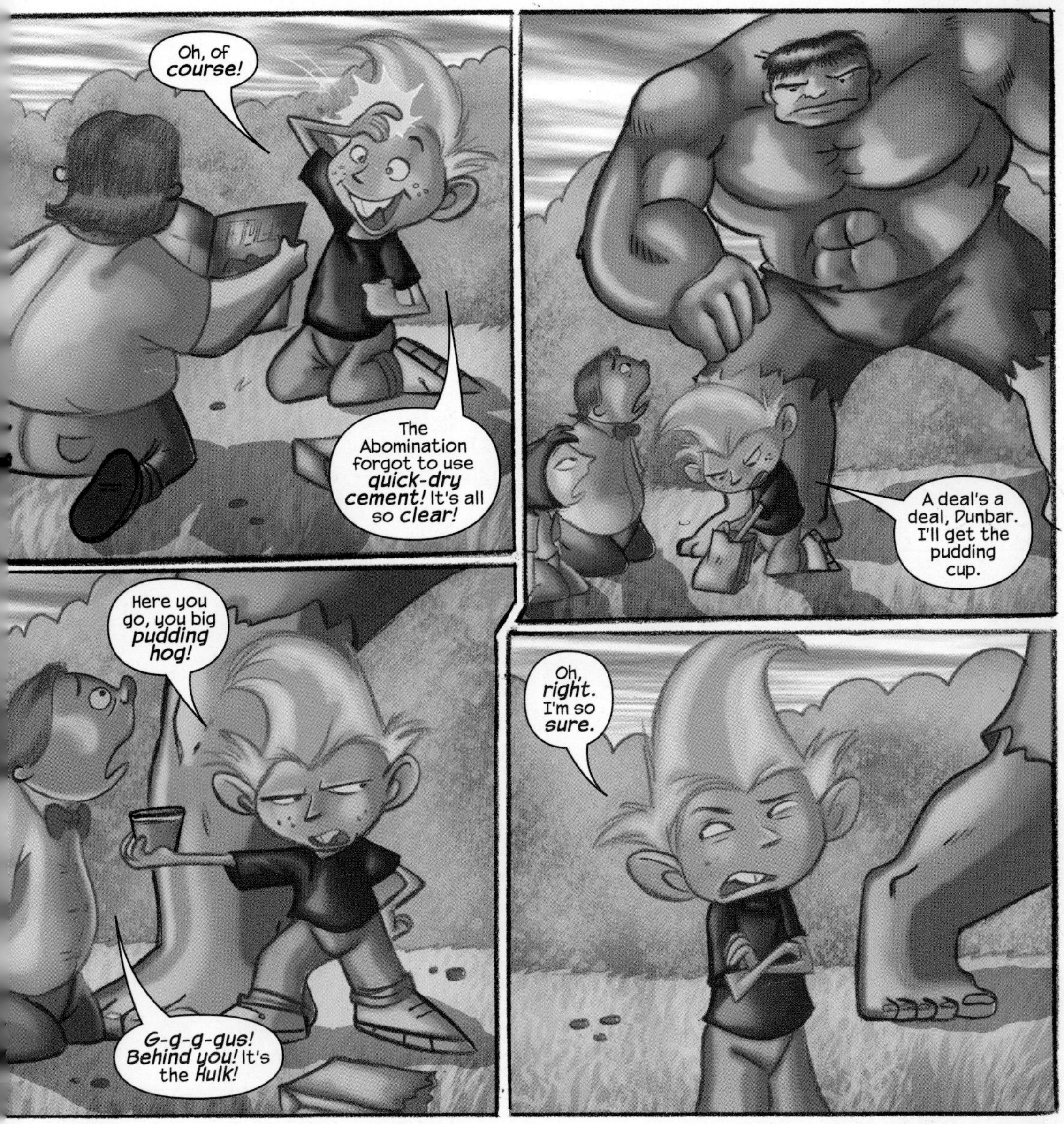
Oh, of course!
The Abomination forgot to use quick-dry cement! It's all so clear!
A deal's a deal, Dunbar. I'll get the pudding cup.
Here you go, you big pudding hog!
G-g-g-gus! Behind you! It's the Hulk!
Oh, right. I'm so sure.

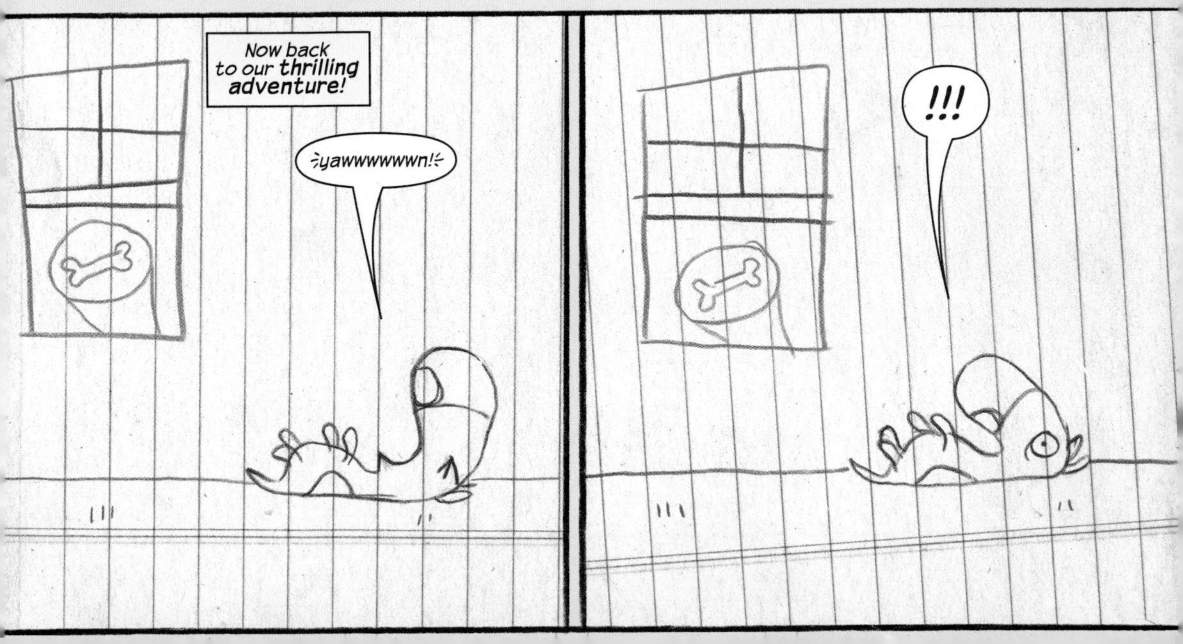
Now back to our thrilling adventure!
yawwwwwwn!
!!!

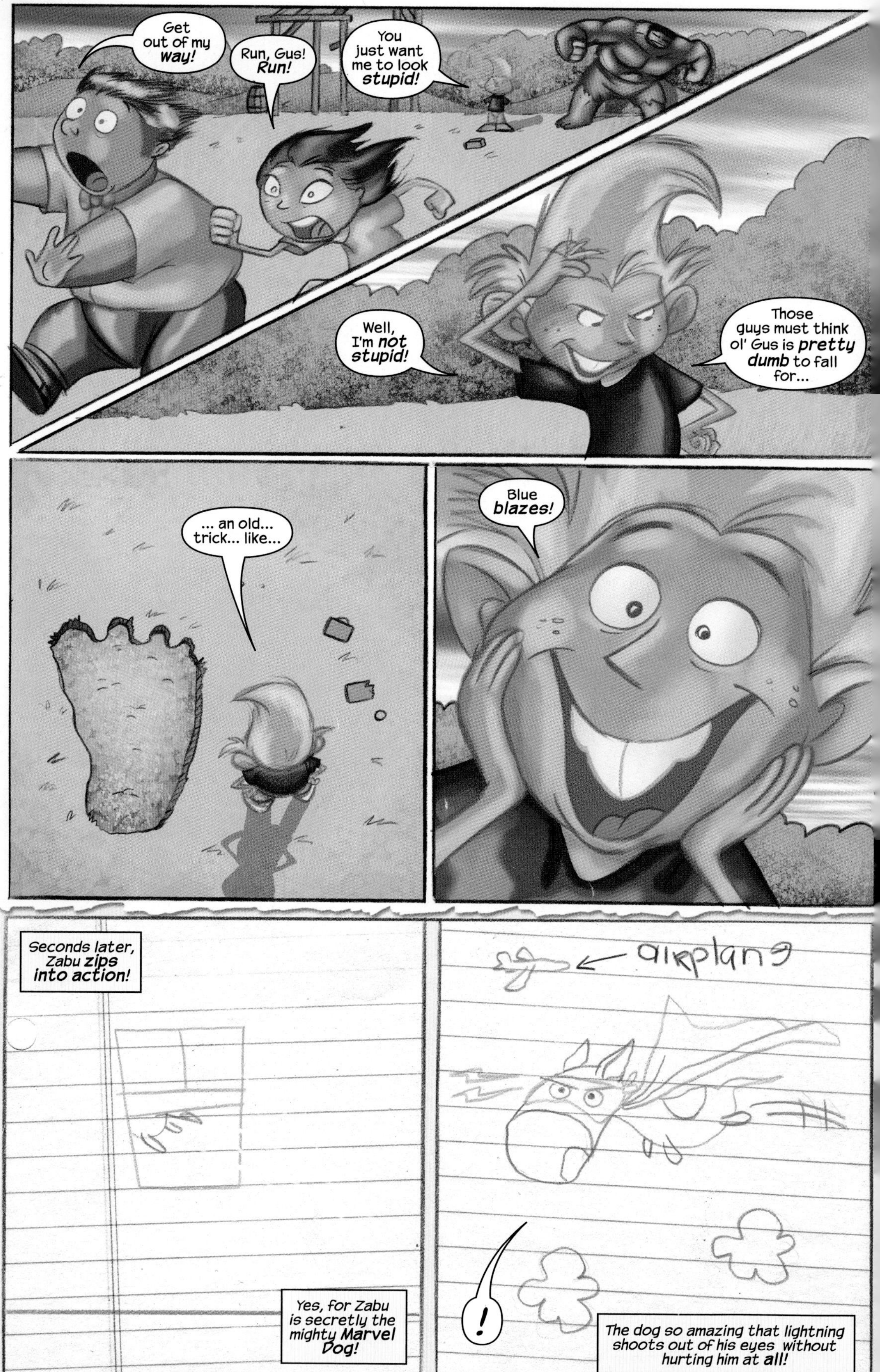
Get out of my way!
Run, Gus! Run!
You just want me to look stupid!
Well, I'm not stupid!
Those guys must think ol' Gus is pretty dumb to fall for...
... an old... trick... like...
Blue blazes!
Seconds later, Zabu zips into action!
Yes, for Zabu is secretly the mighty Marvel Dog!
airplane
!
The dog so amazing that lightning shoots out of his eyes without hurting him at all!

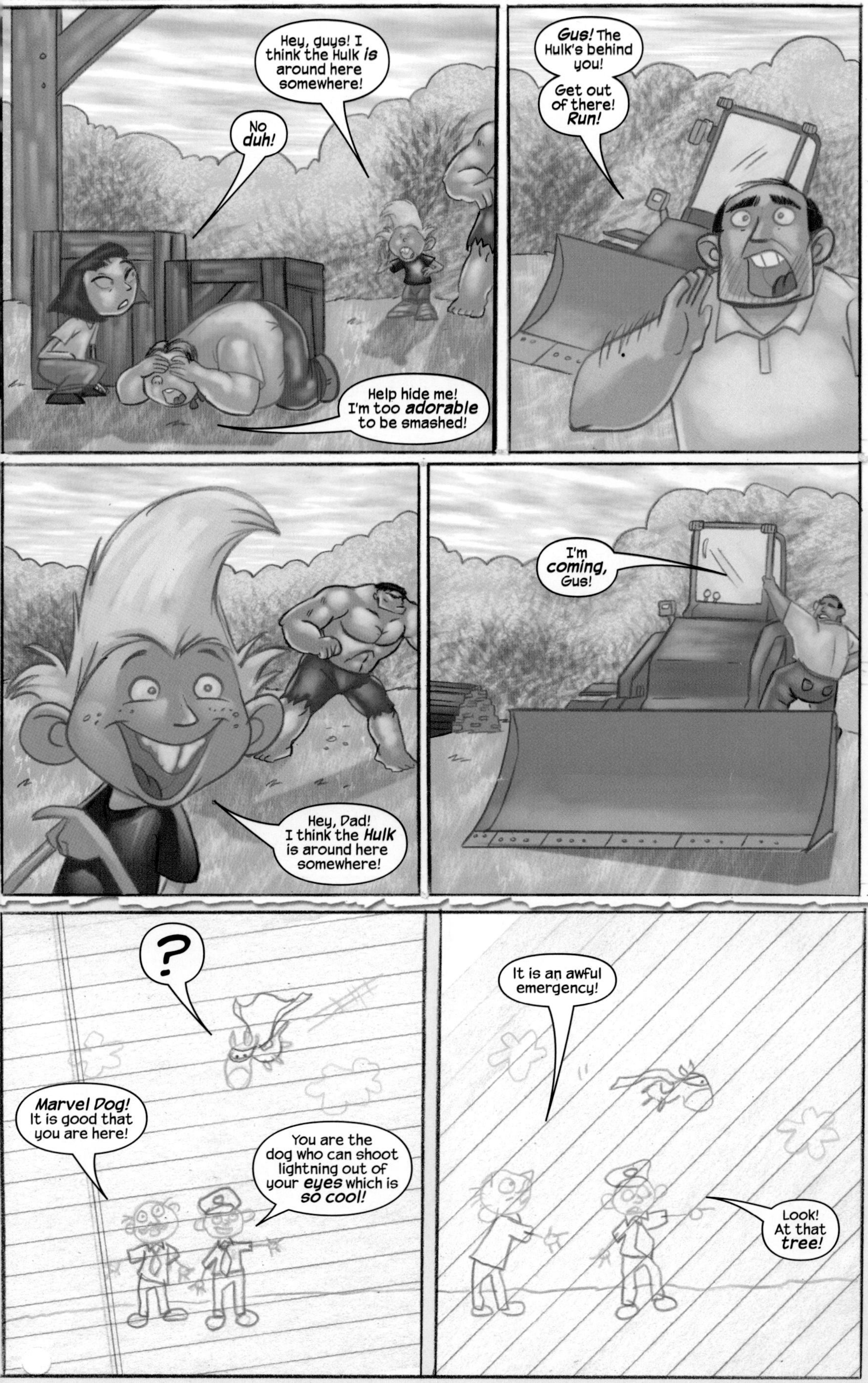
Hey, guys! I think the Hulk *is* around here somewhere!
No *duh!*
Help hide me! I'm too *adorable* to be smashed!
Gus! The Hulk's behind you!
Get out of there! *Run!*
Hey, Dad! I think the *Hulk* is around here somewhere!
I'm *coming,* Gus!
?
Marvel Dog! It is good that you are here!
You are the dog who can shoot lightning out of your *eyes* which is *so cool!*
It is an awful emergency!
Look! At that *tree!*

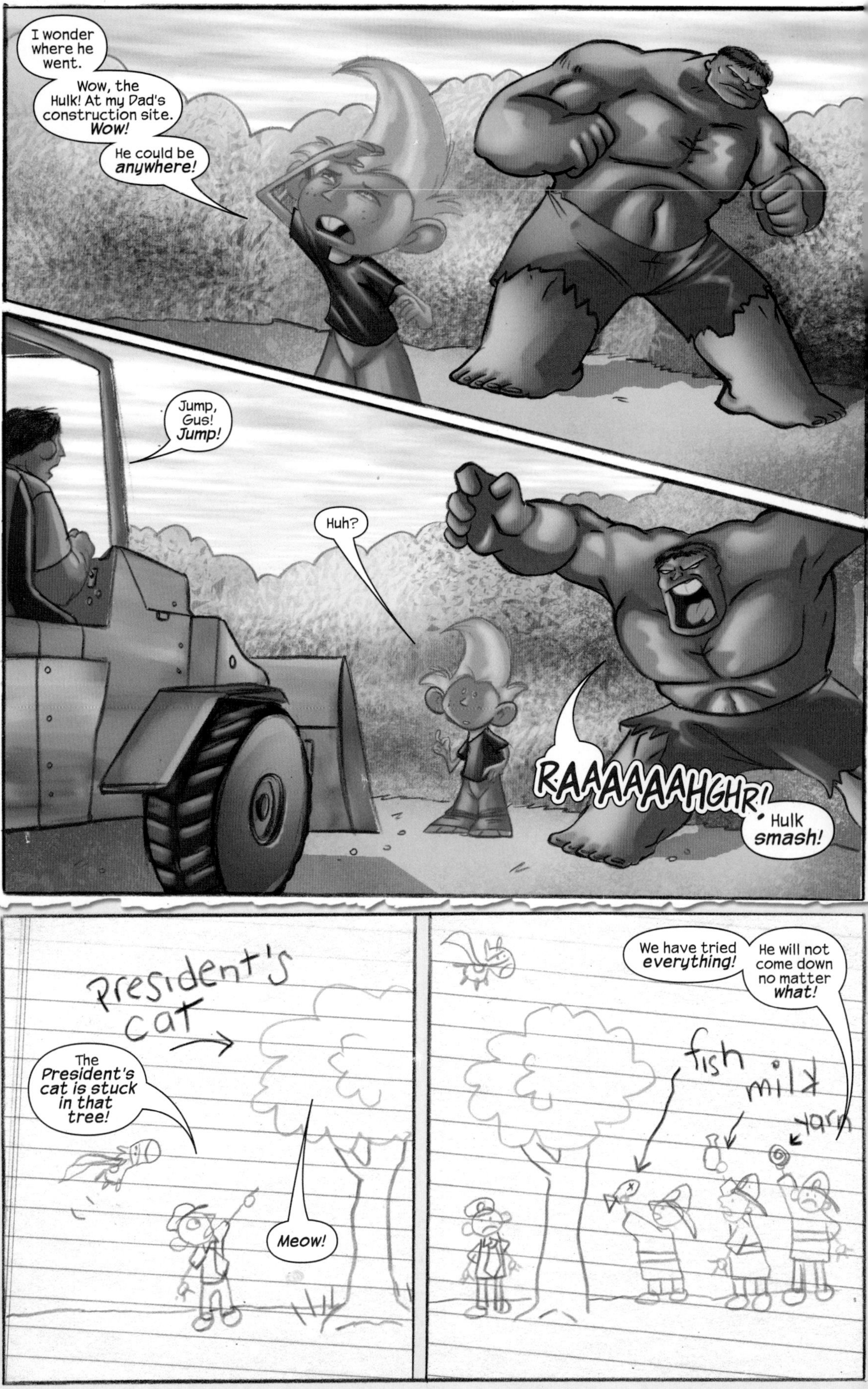
I wonder where he went.
Wow, the Hulk! At my Dad's construction site. *Wow!*
He could be *anywhere!*
Jump, Gus! *Jump!*
Huh?
RAAAAAAHGHR!
Hulk *smash!*
President's cat
The *President's cat is stuck in that tree!*
Meow!
We have tried *everything!*
He will not come down no matter *what!*
fish
milk
yarn

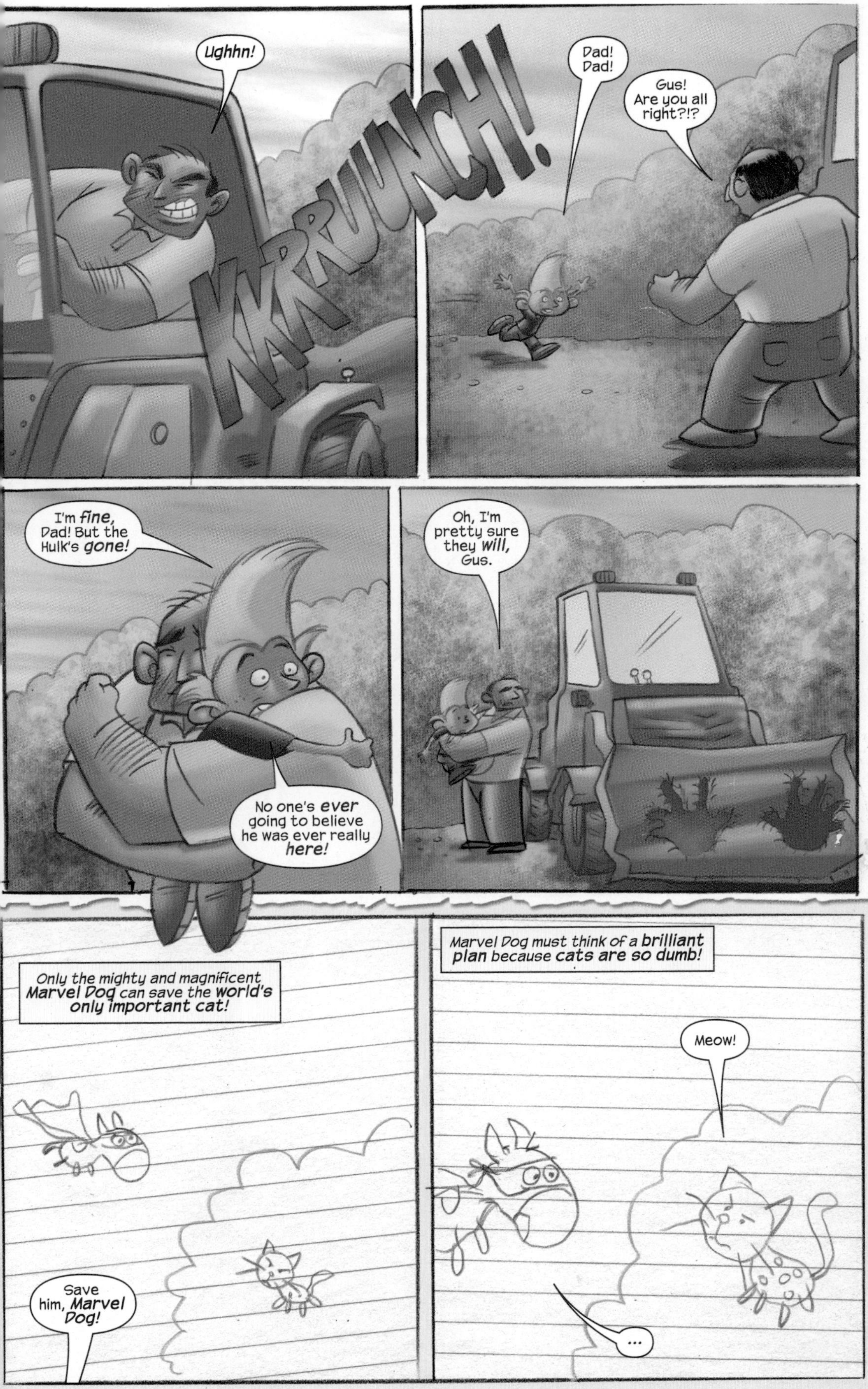
Ughhn!
KKRRUUNCH!
Dad! Dad!
Gus! Are you all right?!?
I'm fine, Dad! But the Hulk's gone!
No one's ever going to believe he was ever really here!
Oh, I'm pretty sure they will, Gus.
Only the mighty and magnificent Marvel Dog can save the world's only important cat!
Save him, Marvel Dog!
Marvel Dog must think of a brilliant plan because cats are so dumb!
Meow!
...

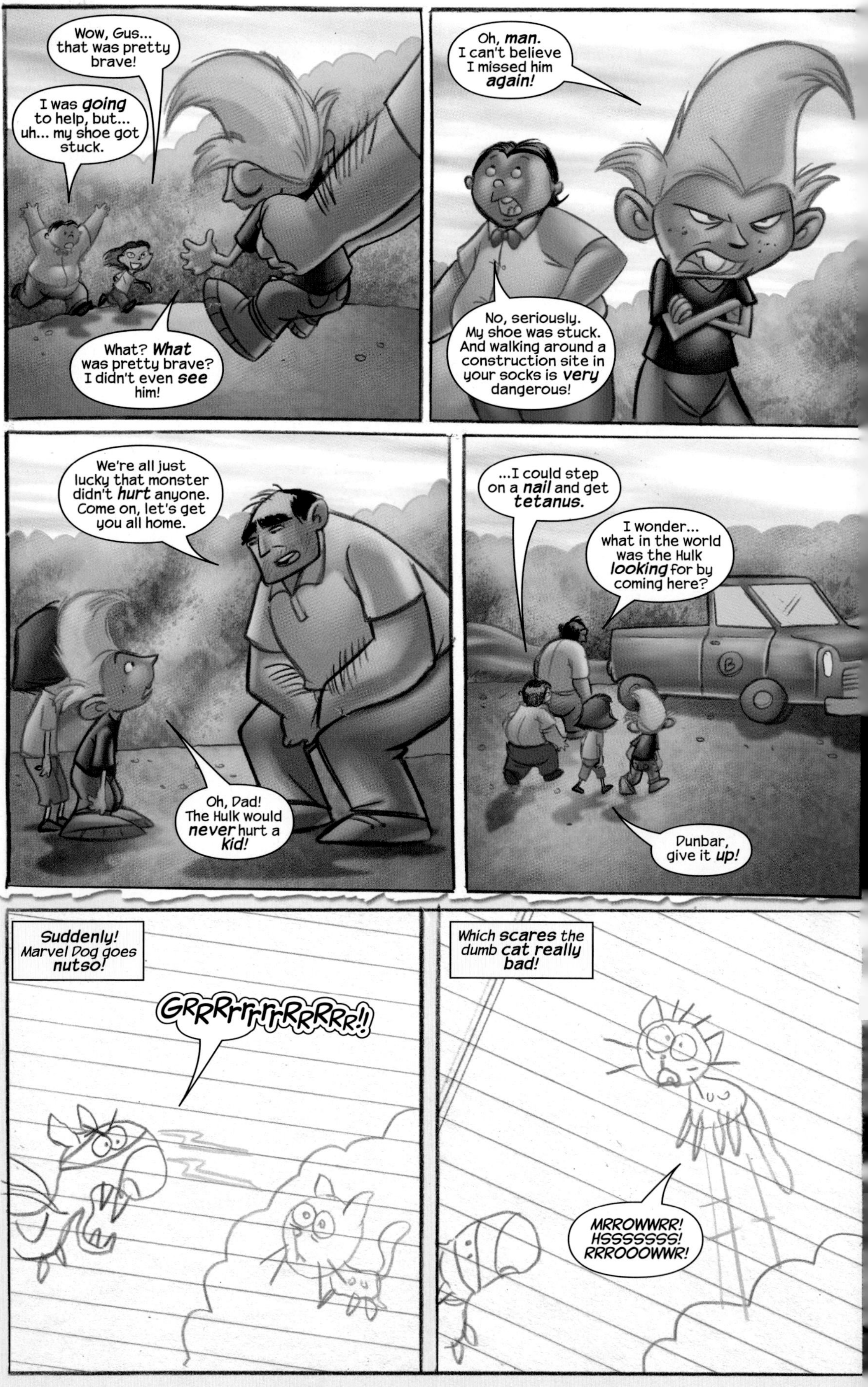
Wow, Gus... that was pretty brave!
I was going to help, but... uh... my shoe got stuck.
What? What was pretty brave? I didn't even see him!
Oh, man. I can't believe I missed him again!
No, seriously. My shoe was stuck. And walking around a construction site in your socks is very dangerous!
We're all just lucky that monster didn't hurt anyone. Come on, let's get you all home.
Oh, Dad! The Hulk would never hurt a kid!
...I could step on a nail and get tetanus.
I wonder... what in the world was the Hulk looking for by coming here?
Dunbar, give it up!
Suddenly! Marvel Dog goes nutso!
GRRRrrrrrRRRRR!!
Which scares the dumb cat really bad!
MRROWWRR! HSSSSSSS! RRROOOWWR!

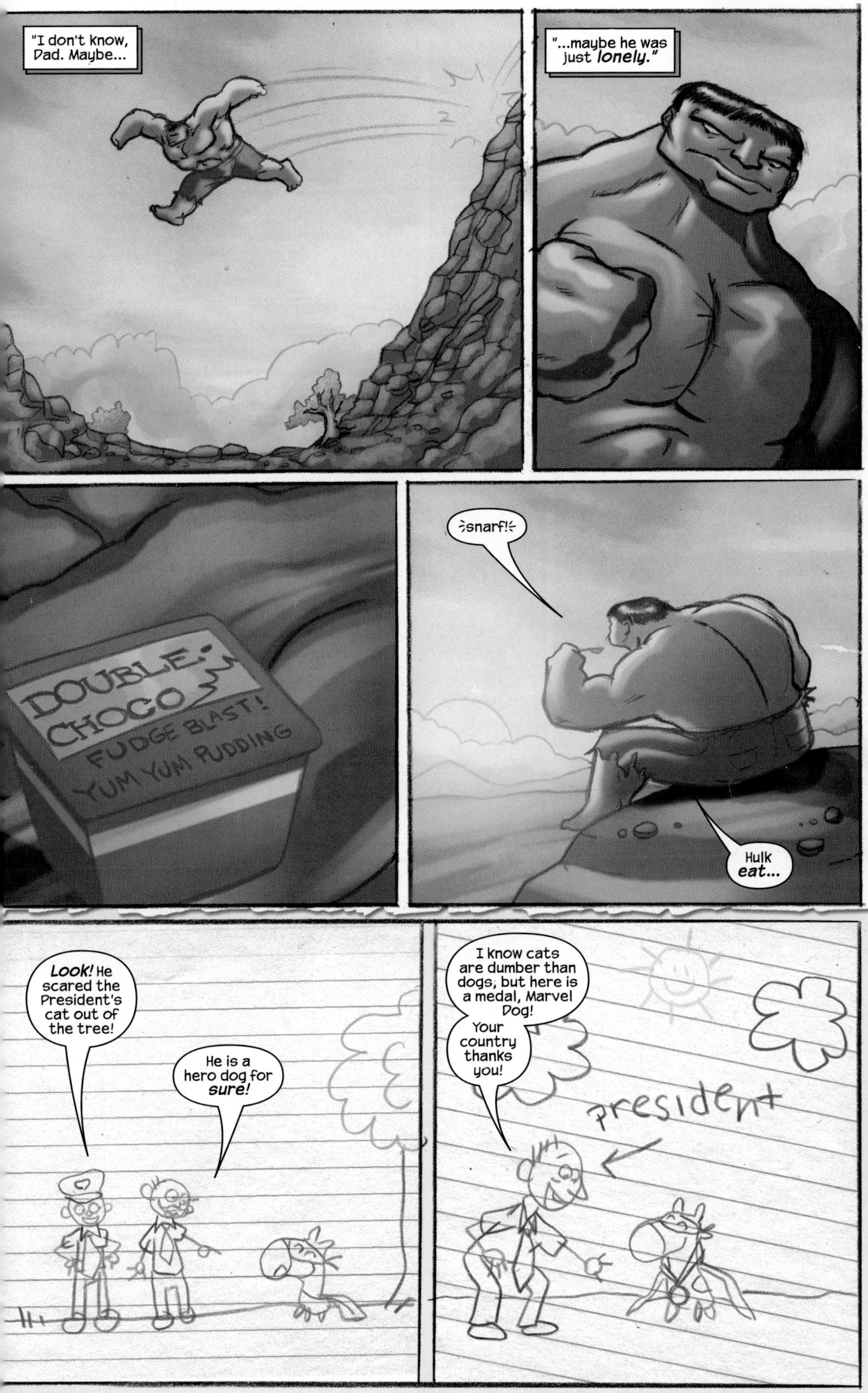
"I don't know, Dad. Maybe...
"...maybe he was just *lonely.*"
DOUBLE-CHOCO FUDGE BLAST! YUM YUM PUDDING
snarf!
Hulk *eat...*
Look! He scared the President's cat out of the tree!
He is a hero dog for *sure!*
I know cats are dumber than dogs, but here is a medal, Marvel Dog!
Your country thanks you!
President

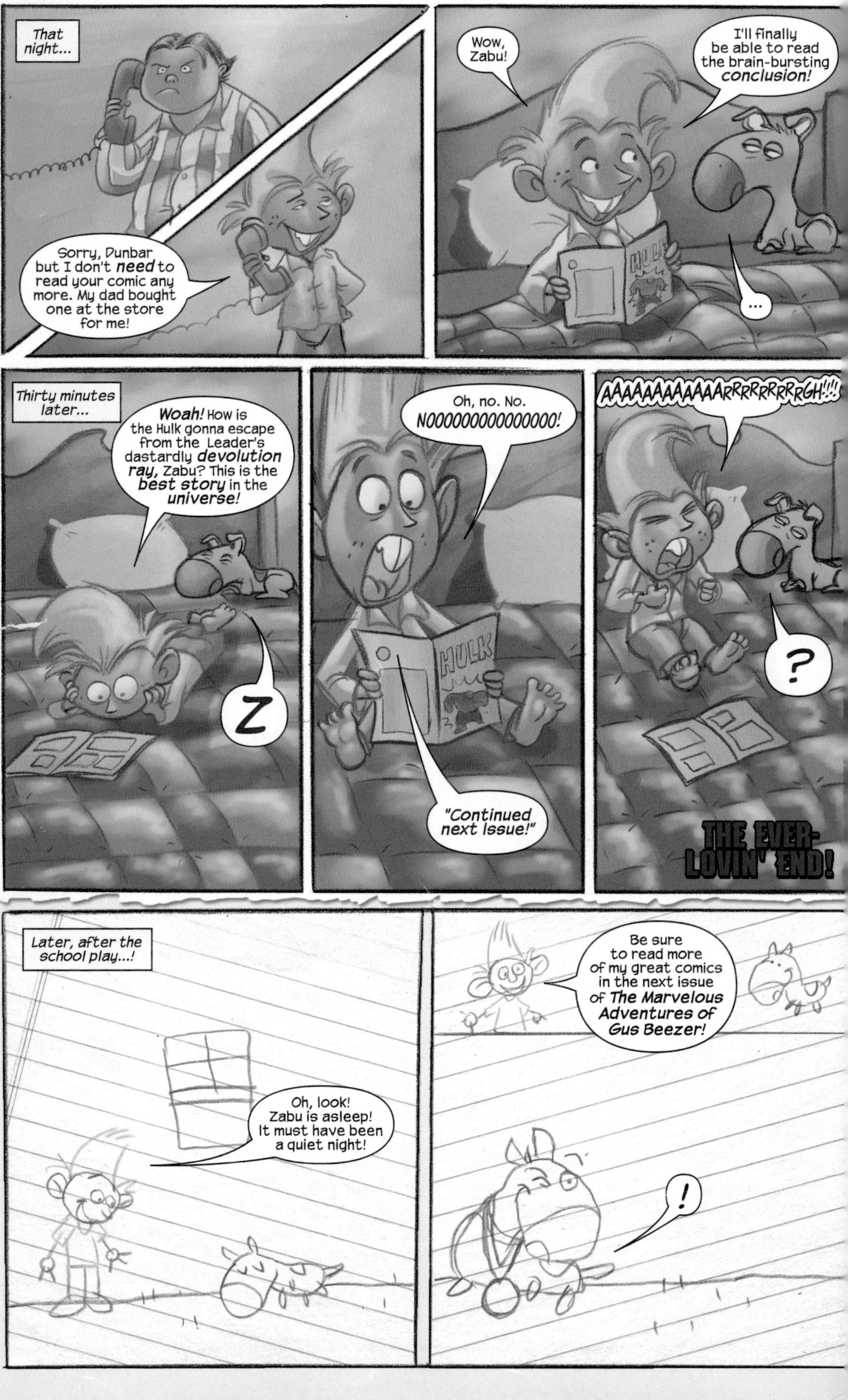
That night...
Sorry, Dunbar but I don't *need* to read your comic any more. My dad bought one at the store for me!
Wow, Zabu!
I'll finally be able to read the brain-bursting *conclusion!*
...
Thirty minutes later...
Woah! How is the Hulk gonna escape from the Leader's dastardly *devolution ray,* Zabu? This is the *best story* in the *universe!*
Z
Oh, no. No. NOOOOOOOOOOOOOO!
"Continued next Issue!"
AAAAAAAAAAAARRRRRRRRGH!!!!
?
THE EVER-LOVIN' END!
Later, after the school play...!
Oh, look! Zabu is asleep! It must have been a quiet night!
Be sure to read more of my great comics in the next issue of *The Marvelous Adventures of Gus Beezer!*
!